AMATEUR GUN PLAY

ED GENTLE

WORKBOOK PRESS LLC
187 E Warm Springs Rd,
Suite B285, Las Vegas, NV 89119, USA

Website: https://workbookpress.com/
Hotline: 1-888-818-4856
Email: admin@workbookpress.com

Ordering Information:
Quantity sales. Special discounts are available on quantity purchases by corporations, associations, and others.
For details, contact the publisher at the address above.

ISBN-13:   978-1-958176-00-9 (Paperback Version)
                  978-1-958176-01-6 (Digital Version)

REV. DATE: 29/03/2022

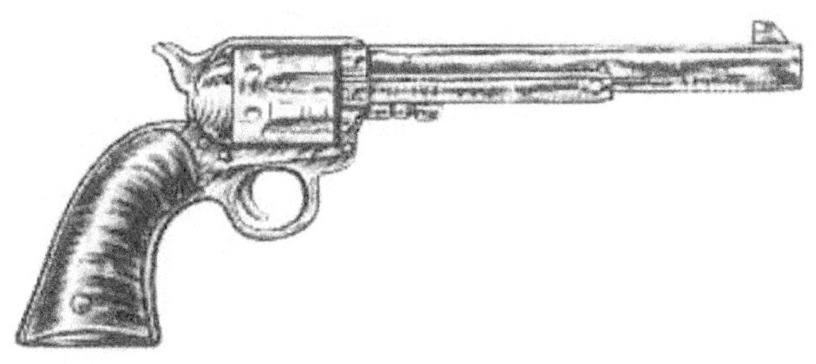

AMATEUR GUN PLAY

These 10 stories describe the effects of guns on our lives. Guns interface with love, common sense, ethics, money, politics and other aspects of being human.

There are 20,000 gun deaths per year in the United States. This figure does not take into account all the gun encounters without a fatality. 10 close encounters with guns in a lifetime is not unusual.

Ironically, at these barrel of a gun moments, lives are often reset. Many times, a fast-paced western world slows down, and reflection on the meaning of life takes place, sometimes in an instant. Sometimes for a lifetime if you survive. This instrument of death can change a life, even improve one. Or, it can mean the end.

The stories are fictitious but are grounded in truth.

Ed Gentle

ABOUT THE AUTHOR

Ed Gentle is 68 and has 5 college degrees, 3 in law. He lives with his family in Birmingham, Alabama, where he practices law.

SO YOU CAN LOOK HIM IN THE EYES

Bobby was a murder suspect.

Bobby went to college at the University of Georgia and studied mechanical engineering, a very difficult course. To make ends meet, he had a roommate and three jobs, supporting a girlfriend and their son. Bobby's college roommate, Randy, also majored in engineering.

Bobby and Randy went back. They were both over 6 feet and had played high school football in Georgia, playing each other a couple of times. Bobby was now on the college football team, but he described his position as "tackle dummy." Randy no longer played football but did play rugby, with Bobby joining him occasionally. Neither was a drinker, both were quiet. Neither seemed to be the person who would snap.

Randy had recently separated from his wife, Glenda. Glenda liked a dentist. Randy and his wife soon divorced, but the problem did not end. The dentist, Dr. Walker, and the ex-wife would call Randy at night while they were having sex to drive him crazy. He lamented to Bobby and said he would kill them both.

Here is a typical call from the wife and dentist.

"Randy, it's me. I bet you are all alone. I'm never alone, thanks to my favorite dentist here."

"Randy, this is Dr. Walker. I'm filling your wife's holes in a very special way. Can't you hear me drilling?'

"Coo's, screams, and oh yes."

Click.

After dentist and wife hung up, they often called 30 minutes later and told Randy they were repeating the process and hoped he was enjoying it.

These episodes began to get to Randy. He wondered why Dr. Walker and Glenda would harass him for their own pleasure. What had he done to merit this abuse? He thought it probably was originated by the dentist, thinking that doctors are well educated and sometimes have a mean streak. What was in it for Glenda?

This went on for some time. The more it upset Randy the happier the dentist and the former spouse seemed to be. They became more and more graphic in their phone calls, and Randy's suffering made it hard for Bobby to study.

Finally, one night after receiving explicit dirty talk on the phone, Randy asked Bobby what he should do. Bobby said I would strangle them both so you can look them in the eyes. This seemed to satisfy Randy, and Bobby could finish his homework while Randy was asleep.

Once the threshold of discussing murder was crossed, Randy would not stop talking. Bobby wondered how this could be the same peaceful person he had known in high school, but there was no going back. Randy talked about murdering the dentist and his ex-wife dozens of times, scheming about shooting them, catching them both in bed and using chloroform, burning the dentist's house with them in it after securing the doors and windows from the outside, waiting for them in the morning to shoot them in their cars, and so on. Bobby played along to try to keep Randy quiet, so Bobby could do his homework.

The murder talk then escalated to drive-by's. Randy would drive-by the dentist's house and his ex-wife's house, to see whose car was where. He would ask Bobby to come along, and Bobby often did.

College life went on, Bobby studied and still held down a few jobs to take care of his young son. Randy would try to study, would get his phone calls about mid-evening, and then get off key. Bobby tried to time his work so that he was in bed asleep by the time of the call. A routine developed, and Bobby hoped it would stick.

To save money after Bobby's girlfriend moved out, Ralph, a third roommate joined Randy and Bobby. Bobby was thankful because Randy's harangue was now shared by two. Ralph was more cooperative than Bobby, and would faithfully travel with Randy at night to check on the dentist and the ex-wife.

Then, one evening, something changed. The calls from the dentist and the ex-wife did not come in. Randy announced that he was not expecting them. But according to Randy, "I have made Peace with Glenda and Dr. Walker. Bobby thought, "good" and didn't ask Randy what had happened.

This time of quiet continued for about a month.

A couple of days later Randy was caught with the two bodies in the trunk of his car and placed in custody. When asked by the Athens, Georgia Sheriff what he had done, he described the problem with his wayward wife and the dentist, and said he strangled them both because Bobby told him he could "look them in the eyes".

The local Sheriff tried to work up what had happened. Apparently, Ralph had gone with Randy to the dentist's house and found the dentist and ex-wife together in bed. While Ralph waited outside, Randy shot them both in bed, with the dentist screaming loud enough for Ralph to hear, "are you crazy Randy!!!" and the ex crying. As the life left their bodies, Randy strangled them both with nylon rope. Though Ralph did not help kill them, he did help Randy clean up and try to hide the evidence.

Ralph agreed to tell the whole story to the Sheriff for immunity.

With Randy in jail, Bobby also became a murder conspiracy suspect. A Sheriff's Deputy began to hang out with Bobby. He showed up for breakfast, followed Bobby to class, and even sometimes slept over. Bobby adopted him, like he did with everyone else, and they became friends. Finally, the Deputy gave up.

Randy was indicted and tried for double murder. He was assigned a Public Defender who didn't spend much time with his case. Bobby was subpoenaed as a witness.

When Bobby was put on the stand, he was asked fairly vanilla questions about being Randy's roommate, and whether Randy interacted much with the victims. When Bobby tried to elaborate on what happened and why, stressing the nightly phone calls, he was shouted down by the Judge. This was very frustrating, because Bobby thought there was a great reason for the double murders.

Randy was convicted and given 25 years with a chance of parole in 5. After 5 years, though not paroled, Randy was allowed to work at a McDonalds during the day and then go back to jail at night. Randy wrote Bobby a few times, asking if Bobby would come see him at the McDonalds, but Bobby ignored him. In the letters Randy would claim to miss Glenda. Bobby wondered if Randy missed the phone calls, the opportunity to murder her or what.

Finally, 10 years after incarceration, Randy was given parole. He called Bobby and asked if Bobby would like to hang out. Bobby said, "no".

Thinking the ex-wife must be a Helen of Troy, whose beauty launched 1,000 ships, I asked Bobby what the ex had looked like, "Ugly", very ugly," he said.

BROTHERLY LOVE

Jack and Chris were born with silver spoons in their mouths. They were the two sons of L.J., who owned a marina on Wharton Lake, on the Alabama Georgia border.

L.J. put Wharton Lake on the map. When it flooded in the 1960s and brimmed with crappie, L.J. spread the word far and wide. He appeared at boat shows throughout the South and used his booming voice and charming personality to attract fishermen. Fishing on the lake became brisk, especially in the Spring and Fall when the crappie were running. Soon, Wharton Lake was called the Crappie Capitol of the World. L.J.'s marina grew likewise.

The L.J. family prospered, clearing about a million a year.

Under the Hapsburg Effect, many times a successful parent does not pass on prosperity to the child. That happened here.

With their Dad bringing in the money, Chris and Jack goofed off. Chris was a mechanic in the boat shop at the marina, but never got "certified", so he never made much money. Jack was a bass bum. He would fish as much as he could. One time he bragged that he had fished 100 days in a row. Their Dad gave them each a "allowance", and life rocked along.

I remember, when I was a young fisherman, Jack would sit at the dock at the marina and beg for someone to take him out fishing, even though he was not even a teenager.

Jack knew every inch and brush pile at Wharton Lake. He dominated bass tournaments, seeming to know each bass by name.

All good things end. L.J. came down with cancer one cold February morning. At the time, Jack was fishing a bass tournament and did not find out until that afternoon. The funeral was well attended, and we all congratulated Chris and Jack at their fortune of owning a marina together. When L.J. died he had $600,000 in CDs.

Unfortunately, Chris and Jack were not good friends. Chris at least pretended to work and was 5'9". Jack never pretended and was 6'2". Somehow, Chris could bully Jack.

After L.J., the marina and its store languished. Slowly, Chris and Jack tried to put the management back together and the marina fumbled forward. Because of its unique location on Wharton Lake, the marina still prospered. There were perhaps two other competing marinas in the whole lake of 30,000 acres.

Chris found himself running the marina and store with Jack frolicking on the lake. Jack, however, when he came in from fishing, would stop by the marina and dip into the cash register.

Chris commented that if Jack wanted to be paid, he needed to work. Chris did this first in a joking manner, and then more and more seriously, as the erosion of the till threatened payroll.

Finally, on St. Patrick's Day, there was a confrontation. Chris told Jack that Jack couldn't take any money and Jack did any way. Chris caught Jack in a stranglehold, and hit him with the baseball bat under the counter, cracking his skull. Jack reached for the Glock pistol also under the counter and shot Chris in the leg.

Lucky me, I was in Kansas visiting one of my sons and got a call that morning from Jack.

Jack said, "I shot my brother."

I said, "Did you kill him?"

Jack said, "No, but I should have."

I told Jack to get an ambulance ASAP and to apologize to his brother, which he refused to do.

An amazing fisherman, Jack won a bass tournament that Saturday, despite a cracked skull.

Matters went down hill after that. Lots of fishermen continued to use the marina, including me. We tried our best to put our boats in, have a little breakfast, fish and leave without getting in the crossfire.

Chris and Jack each got lawyers and the marina was sold at auction for half its value. The brothers split their monies, about $300,000 each.

The drama, however, was not quite over. Jack was indicted for assault and battery for shooting Chris, and given a 3 year paroled sentence.

That did not stop Jack from attacking his brother again. The next time, Jack was put in the county jail. When Jack's lawyer visited him, Jack didn't realize that all conversations were monitored.

Jack said, "I'm going to kill Judge Bryce, for putting me here."

His lawyer said, "Please stop, they can hear you."

It was too late. Judge Bryce then refused to give Jack bail and he spent Thanksgiving and Christmas in jail.

To make his family feel better, I gave his wife a turkey for Thanksgiving and a ham for Christmas.

When Jack went on trial, the Judge extended Jack's parole a couple more years and banned Jack from Wharton Lake and the counties where it was located. Jack therefore moved to a neighboring lake where he guides to this day.

Chris did not quite feel that things were even.

Mysteriously, the trailer that Jack had left behind at Wharton Lake and was trying to sell burned one night.

Shortly thereafter, Chris announced that things were even. He did tattoo on his leg, however, just above the bullet wound scar, a tattoo which said, "Brotherly Love."

AFTERMATH

Some of my settlements involve community torts, where a toxin pollutes a neighborhood. Closed Zinc smelter clean ups are an example.

We had one in Pennsylvania on the heels of a very successful jury verdict obtained by a famous national Law Firm. The toxins, cadmium, arsenic, zinc and lead, are obvious health hazards. But, a large share of our claimants either smoke or are obese, so the causation could have been a problem. For some reason, though, Defense Counsel laid down at trial, and didn't have much of a plan. Indeed, they had no experts.

Some of the facts were compelling. 50 years ago, while the smelter was up and running, a fog rolled in and trapped the smoke from the smelter in a valley with many residents. Four died, and many were injured. Even though this had nothing to do with the need for a clean up now, with the smelter having been closed for decades, the Judge let these facts in for the Jury to hear at the trial. The Jury visibly reacted to their presentation.

We took a break in the trial, and tried to mediate a settlement without success. Even with these facts in the minds of the Jury, we couldn't get the number up high enough. So, the case went forward.

After a jury verdict for a few hundred million dollars, we successfully mediated a settlement, which involved a clean up of the soil surrounding the old zinc smelter site and the homes whose attics had dust blown in by the wind over the years in about a 3-mile radius around the now closed plant.

The community just wanted the money and not a cleanup. We therefore gathered together the 10 biggest troublemakers, and made them our claimants committee. Slowly, we sold them on the health benefits of a cleanup and the community relented.

One of our committee members, Dan, was a strong advocate for the cleanup. Large in size and personality, and well loved by all, we called him the Mayor of Dresden, the town where the smelter was located. He encouraged claimants to participate in the cleanup, was Santa Claus at our Christmas parties and helped us replace the mistrust of rural Pennsylvanians for outsiders with a belief that the settlement cleanup would help them and especially their children and grandchildren.

We had an office in the Dresden fire station, and I would stay there two weeks at a time. Rural Pennsylvania can be lonely and dreary, and I called it the Island.

Dan, however, kept me in good cheer. He was an avid musky fisherman. I had never gone musky fishing before. He would show me lures he had carved that were so big you could probably eat them if you didn't catch anything. He was always enthusiastic and positive, even though a musky is the fish of ten thousand casts.

Dan had a mounted 30-lb musky in his house, with one of his homemade lures hanging from its mouth. When we went to see him, he loved to take the lure out of the musky's mouth and talk about successful fishing trips. One, on Pelham Lake, resulted in a fish of a lifetime. Dan claimed that it was a 54-inch fish, which he measured and let go. It would have been the Pennsylvania state record.

Dan and his fishing buddy Rodney adopted me, and we went fishing many times. Rodney pointed out the dead tree in the water where Dan had caught his trophy musky, and Rodney and I would beat that hole every time we would go fishing, but without success. After 20 trips I actually caught one. Obviously, you do not musky fish to catch muskies.

Dan, however, had marital and health problems. His wife left him and he began to drink and eat too much. Rodney and I would visit him frequently, though now he had trouble getting around. He still talked lovingly of fishing, but did not join us any longer.

Rodney fell ill and died of cancer, and I was there only half the time, as the cleanup wound down. A neighbor up the hill, Ludger, was also a friend of Dan's, and took over Dan's dog walking duties.

Ludger was also a clean-up claimant. When we sampled the soil on his property, it did not have enough contamination to be cleaned up. This upset him, because he lived right next to the smelter. Strangely, with clean-ups, contamination does not always follow a set pattern. Sort of like a neighborhood hit by a tornado, with homes leveled, but one being untouched, some properties surrounding the Zinc smelter, for unknown reasons, did not get contaminated. We continued to sample Ludger's property even though we couldn't find any contamination. He began to have as many potholes as the moon. Of course, we filled the holes in and told Ludger he should be happy. Ludger was friendly and would spend the time talking to you, having retired for many years. Indeed, the whole neighborhood was full of retirees, and I tried to do work early and late in order to reduce the amount of talking.

As the cleanup progressed through the town, Dan's house was next on the list. He was a tenant, and was behind in his rent. Dan feared that, if he vacated the house for the cleanup, the landlord would change the locks and not let Dan back in. This was a distinct possibility.

Dan became more and more depressed. Ludger and I confiscated his many weapons, or so we thought.

The week before Dan was scheduled to vacate his house for the cleanup, he took his life and that of his dog with a rifle that he had hidden from us. This was discovered after Ludger and I both had dropped by and knocked on the door with no results.

The fire department pried open the door and found the grisly scene. I wept like a baby and cussed myself for pushing forward with the cleanup at Dan's expense.

At the claims office, one of our assistants was an ex-cop. He suggested that we get Aftermath to clean up the problem. I asked what that was. And he said it specializes in sanitizing crime scenes.

As good a name as any. Rest in peace, Dan. Your legacy of a clean Dresden lives on, as shown by many healthy children and grandchildren. The muskies and I miss you.

NO SAFETY

I have law degrees from England and the United States. The philosophy of legally representing clients in the two nations varies greatly. In England, there is a search for truth. If a lawyer knows that his client is lying, he should tell the Judge. In the United States, we have more of a gun slinger mentality. The lawyer advocates for the client, even if he knows that the client is guilty and liable. Legal confidences are treated differently. In England, if you discover that a crime has been committed by your client, you have a duty to report it to the authorities. In America, you can just withdraw from representing the client and take the secret to your grave. The argument for the English approach is to get to the truth. The argument in America is to protect client confidences.

As a lawyer, I struggle with the American conflicting charges of representing your client zealously while being ethical. In doing so, the result is sometimes flawed. Here are two examples involving guns.

The first case involved a white, right-winged outdoorsman in Lynchburg, Tennessee, who graduated from college with a Wildlife Management degree. He was a biker and a gun collector, and liked to pack.

I knew Nathan for some time, helping him on a previous matter successfully.

One evening at a biker rally, he bent down to retie a boot and his derringer fell out of his pocket. Upon hitting the pavement, it discharged, and shot him in the head.

Nathan was in intensive care for some time, and we did not know if he would survive. He slowly got better but could not speak. After six months of therapy he began to get his wits and his personality back, and began to talk about his case. Nathan understood that the derringer was an inexpensive piece, but it had the safety on and he claimed that the gun was defective. After having an expert look at the gun and express the opinion that the safety was, indeed, ineffective, we filed a lawsuit for Nathan.

The Defendant gun manufacturer had a ferocious Defense Firm, which fought us every step of the way, arguing lack of sound gun precautions by Nathan, and the safety not being on.

Nathan's deposition was taken, and he did a good job. The aggression of the manufacturer was to our advantage in a rural Tennessee town, and both sides agreed to mediate the case.

The mediator did well, getting Nathan $300,000. Because Nathan was still struggling physically, we waived our attorneys' fees, though we had 500 hours in the case.

When Nathan met with us to get his check, he asked to talk to me privately.

Nathan said, "The safety was off you know."

Flabbergasted, I said nothing, but sent a letter to Nathan withdrawing from his case. As a lawyer, I was bound to secrecy, but pretended to keep my dignity.

The other case involved an abusive marriage of a Gadsden, Alabama couple. The husband was known to assault the wife, but she stayed.

The wife called me and reported that her husband's gun had gone off when it was dropped on the floor and shot him in the chest accidentally. He was rushed to the hospital but did not survive.

His now widow provided us with the gun to have an expert inspect it in order to find out why it discharged even though the safety was on.

We took the gun to the expert, who called a week later and asked to meet with me privately. I was beginning to dread these private meetings.

He said, "The gun is not defective. The safety works perfectly."

"In my opinion, the safety was off when the gun discharged."

I thanked the expert and retrieved the gun. Did the wife shoot the husband?

The case was found to be an accident, and no one was prosecuted.

Meeting privately with the wife, I gave her the gun and told her I couldn't take the case. When she asked why, I shared the expert's opinion.

Once again my lips were sealed and I could do nothing.

BIRD BRAIN

Strange things happen when amateurs go hunting. Here are three examples.

In upstate New York, it was spring and turkey season. Hunting for turkeys is a dirty trick. You make a call like a hen, and the male gobbler rushes to you to have sex, and then you shoot him in the head. What a way to go? The danger occurs when one hunter hears another acting like a hen and tries to follow-up on the sound.

In Cooperstown, New York, one Saturday, we heard a shotgun go off in an area where we were headed to hunt. When we got close, we found a dead hunter. Nearby, there were tracks in the snow, and apparent human feces. We called the Game Warden, who investigated the scene.

A sample of the feces was taken, and its DNA was put into the national DNA criminal detection network. Two cousins in New York with similar genes were located. A short interview revealed the apparent culprit, who confessed.

Apparently, as the now deceased hunter approached the murderer, he was mistaken for a turkey and shot to death. The murderer was so upset, he defecated.

In Hattiesburg, Mississippi, bird hunting is king. There are doves and quail clubs, and many expert marksmen. Leon was one of them. He prided himself on being a crack skeet shooter and bird hunter.

I asked to visit him and his son to learn a little bit about this type of sport. A poor shot, I could never do well. I think it is because my eyesight has gotten worse over the years with all the books.

We were hunting a corn field bordering a tree line with a couple of dogs. They successfully located and flushed a few coveys of quail and doves, and I even shot a couple.

One of Leon's birds fell into the lower boughs of a tree and was trapped there, about 8ft off the ground. I suggested to Leon that he not worry about it, but he would not have it.

He tried to use his gun as the bird extraction tool. First, he pushed the barrel toward the bird but could not bust through the heavy canopy to get to the bird. He then flipped the gun over, pushing the stock toward the bird.

The gun went off and shot him in the face. As he died, he said, "Please don't tell anyone I did this."

I was hunting wood ducks with my sister Flo and my Dad when I was in third grade in upstate New York on Mount Pleasant Lake. I waded into the cold water with my Dad's hip boots and put out our 3 wood duck decoys.

Instead of wood ducks, a large canvasback came into the cove toward the decoys.

Flo asked Dad, "Are you going to shoot that eagle?"

Our Dad then shot at the bird and the side of the shotgun blew off, scattering the shot sideways. Fortunately, the shot went to the right and we were all to the left, so no one was hurt. We just lucked out.

Should there be a mandatory gun safety course before purchases of firearms? Kind of like a driver's test before you get your license and get behind the wheel of a car? Even with expertise, though, crazy things happen, as shown with these stories.

CLOSE ENCOUNTERS WITH LEROY AND ALAN

When you administer settlements, you are often on the front line. The lawyers have resolved the case, and have all been paid. You are left with the settlement amount and the requirement that it be divided and paid to the claimants.

The claimants therefore focus on you, and blame you for any delays in being paid or any perceived shortfall in the amount.

This sometimes leads to violence. In the Alabama PCB cases, I had six written death threats. Three from Veterans who can kill you.

Two threats are the most memorable.

Leroy was a claimant in an Alabama town with a toxic tort settlement who sent me a written death threat. Against my recommendation, he was sentenced to six months in prison. His wife, Wanda, was very devoted to him. She would attend periodic town meetings we would have in the Courthouse and would ask if we could let Leroy free so he could go back to work. I explained to her that it was out of my hands.

Then, for one town meeting, Wanda brought a pistol, which was fortunately discovered by the guards when doing the metal detection screening at the Courthouse. When this was brought to my attention, I discussed the matter with Wanda. She claimed that it was just a mistake but, again, asked that Leroy be set free so he could support the family. I wrote a letter to the Judge and asked that this be done. Leroy was released and I never heard anything further.

Alan had the misfortune of being a prisoner in a California jail that blew up and burned. He and about 650 other prisoners experienced resulting personal injury and, for two, even death. One of the high points of the case was the conduct of the male prisoners. The prison had a stairwell in each of its four corners and three were aflame. It had four stories, with females being on the upper two and males being on the lower two.

Some strong male prisoners would not let any males leave down the one operable stairwell until all the women had been evacuated. Heroism in tragedy.

The accident was a perfect storm. The prison was constructed on a lower dip on a flood plain. Clothes driers were on the bottom floor and ran on natural gas. They were not bolted down. When a once in fifty-year rain occurred, there was a 10-foot wall of water that swept through the building. The driers began to float, collided and exploded. In addition to the two prisoners that were killed, two were saved by prisoners holding their heads up above water until they could be extracted from under the driers with some Jaws-of-Life equipment.

When I was asked to administer this case, I suggested that sentences be commuted based upon the degree of injury, because the money, as almost always, was short. This was rebuffed by the powers that be.

Alan was released from prison, having served his time. He began to attend the hearings when the allocation of the settlement recovery among the prisoners was discussed. He cleaned up well, looking like a lawyer. He was also well spoken.

Then some concerning things happened. First, he fired his lawyers. Then, he began to write threatening letters to me. He also drafted a lawsuit against President Trump and me, asking for $10 million.

The camel's back was broken when he drove from a neighboring state to my office and demanded to see me. We reported the incident to the Police, who escorted him off the premises.

We have now determined and paid Alan's recovery. He was vehemently dissatisfied. However, we explained in a couple of letters that there is nothing we can do at this point.

So far, we have heard nothing further from Alan. Hopefully this will stay as much as it did for Leroy.

Is there any way to get around these threats in administering settlements? Probably not. It pays to be careful, though. In the PCB cases, we took the name labels off of our parking spaces at the Law Firm. I was also instructed by the FBI to take different routes between home and work and to make my hours of commuting irregular. A locked front door and a buzzer at the office, with a video camera, are mandatory.

POLITICAL HEAT

When you go to law school, you think that law is about law. Often, though, it is about power and ego. This seems especially true when politics is involved. As a tender lawyer doing legal work at state agencies, I sometimes encountered events like the below.

Before the deregulation of utilities, and continuing for some utilities like electricity, the State Public Service Commission decide whether the utility makes money or not. This concentration of power tempts utilities to come close to and sometimes go over the ethical line.

Bozo was a Public Service Commissioner in Missouri. When he wanted to get serious with a representative of a utility, he would take a derringer from the drawer in his desk, and smack it on the top of the desk and say, "Let's talk seriously now."

Charlie, the State PR person for the telephone company, was caught in a vice by Bozo. Bozo smacked his derringer on his desk, and told Charlie that the phone company needed to install soft drink and candy vending machines in state buildings, with Bozo to get the money. Reluctantly, Charlie agreed.

This indirect binding arrangement went on without a hitch for three years. Then, an activist named Greenie was hired by the Commission. Greenie was keen on finding and eradicating corruption. He would roll himself up in the blankets used in the freight elevators to haul furniture, and sleep until the middle of the night. Then he would roam around the Commission offices and rifle through peoples' drawers. Greenie also liked to tape conversations unknown to the speakers, be it on the phone or in person.

Greenie unearthed the Bozo vending machine plan. He also found a prostitution ring that was being enjoyed by the Commissioners and public utility representatives alike.

At the same time, the phone companies began to have "900 service", which was often dial-a-porn. Greenie went to talk with the Missouri Attorney General, and they came up with a plan. They would indict the telephone companies, including MCI, AT&T, Sprint, and so on. Then, they would put agents on flights that traveled through Missouri airspace and arrest officers of utilities at the appropriate time.

This scheme worked, and two utility officers were so arrested.

Greenie's reform efforts did not end there. Bozo went to prison for three years. His partner in crime, Commissioner Juanita, served two years for double entering travel expenses.

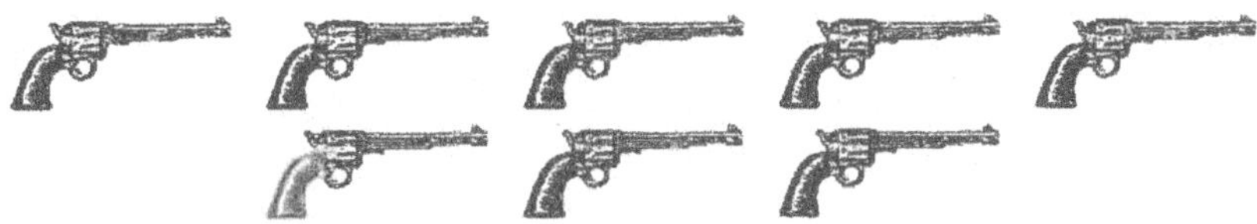

SO DO WE!

Law sometimes is like bananas. Similar cases come in bunches. As we were winding up the Pennsylvania closed Zinc smelter case, another one appeared in Kansas. This time the Defendants hired us to administer the settlement, instead of the Plaintiffs. These Defendants had savvy counsel, having cut their teeth on railroad litigation settlements. They learned to take the heat out of the case by settling with the claimants early. Following a train wreck, a pay station would be set up the next day with releases on the backs of checks. Claimants would get in line and negotiate their settlement amount. They were so happy with this situation and so anxious to be paid, that fist fights sometimes broke out.

This way, the railroad could use hundred percent of dollars instead of giving a third or half of it to plaintiff lawyers. This same approach was taken by some of the same lawyers in the BP Settlement. Ken Feinberg was hired as the Special Master, and used $25 billion to pay direct compensation to claimants, taking a lot of the heat out of the case.

In the Hiawatha, Kansas zinc smelter Settlement, the defendants had done the same. The Plaintiffs' lawyers, being foreigners from Missouri, were not familiar with the community. They made the mistake of not setting up a claims office and befriending community leaders. The defendant, together with its savvy lawyers, began to take the heat out of the case by remediating the town for the claimants free of charge.

By the time the case settled, and we were asked to administer the result, half the town had been cleaned up. The Plaintiff lawyers claimed a third of the gross recovery even though the claimants had not seen much of them. This further incensed the town, and many claimants opted out of the Settlement.

By the time we arrived on the scene, 25% of the claimants had vacated the Settlement, and it was folding. This was another "win back" case. Using our community settlement model, we set up an office in town immediately and hired three locals to run it with a staff member from our office, with staff members to rotate every two weeks. We also identified the nine biggest troublemakers and made them our claimants committee.

I spent much time on the ground, taking the claimants committee fishing or, to the vaunted Kansas college basketball games, while also having spa days for the female members of the committee.

Slowly, we convinced the committee that we were interested in cleaning up the town, for the benefit of the claimants and generations to come. Our subsequent win back program reduced the opt-outs to 5% and the settlement then proceeded.

As always happens, claimants were very anxious to be paid. In this case, they received a payment when their property was cleaned. As Christmas approached, the claimants began to push to be paid.

To take the heat out, we had a Christmas town meeting, and I stayed until every question was answered. This took two days. Even though they were estranged from the claimants, I asked the plaintiff lawyers to attend the town meeting. They hesitantly agreed.

The claimants haranguing of the plaintiff lawyers was embarrassing. One infamous claimant, who had to make a $100 deposit each time he went into a bar to pay for damage, threatened the plaintiff lawyers with violence, and asked them to step outside to get their due reward. Another claimant asked for the legal fees back.

As for all town meetings, we had a law enforcement presence. As the tenor of the meeting escalated, one outspoken plaintiff lawyer, who we nicknamed Rod Stewart because he looked like him, stated that "Everyone needs to simmer down. You know that we have Deputies with guns in the back of the room."

The Chairman of our claimants committee then stood up and announced, "So do we. We are packing too." He had bragged of having 63 weapons and was sometimes irascible. We took him seriously.

At that point, I took the plaintiff lawyers aside, wished them Merry Christmas and suggested that they leave the building. This, they gladly did, to raucous cheers and applause from the claimants and their families. The town never saw them again.

After this episode, an era of "good feeling" pervaded the community. We were like the Pied Piper, having run the lawyers out of town.

The clean up was completed in three years, we made fast friends with the claimants committee and most of the claimants, and I still return to visit from time to time.

Sometimes I wonder if the practice of law is worthwhile. Then I remember the Hiawatha zinc smelter settlement, and all of the properties now cleansed of contaminants.

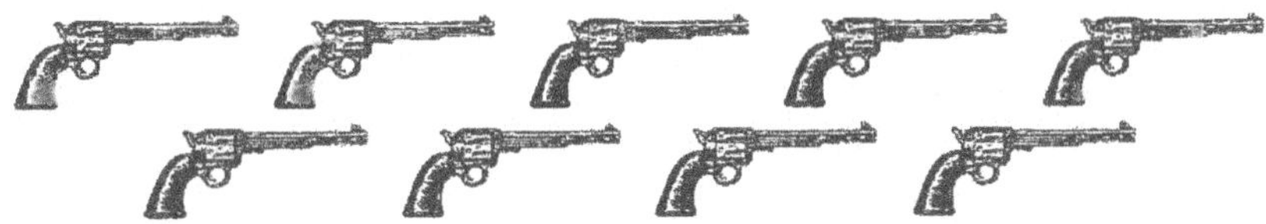

SHERIFF RE-ELECTION TIME AT THE UNIVERSITY OF GEORGIA

At 68 I'm on the Auburn campus this perfect fall day in 2021, as my alma mater, Georgia, continues to dominate college football this year. Walking down West Glenn Street, I notice an apartment house on the left in brick and white trim that looks very much like where I stayed at Georgia my senior year. That was 50 years ago, when I was an athlete and a scholar and weighed 150 pounds soaking wet. Now at 210, I can only sleep in one comfortable position, use an inhaler to breath, and take a handful of pills twice a day. Funny how time gets away.

I only lived in a handful of places the four years that I went to Georgia. First, I had a roommate who ran the 440. He went on to Georgetown his sophomore year, because Georgia only of one year of Russian. I lived without a roommate a couple of years until I found a cheaper place. It was inexpensive for a reason. It was rundown and somewhat drug invested. However, during the day, it was relatively quiet, and I studied all the time when I wasn't running. I stayed at this boarding house until the last winter semester at Georgia when I was forced to leave.

I felt the heat of a Sheriff running for re-election in a close race in Athens. One morning, a few Deputies rounded up about 50 students on drug possession charges. Unfortunately, the boarding house had some of the target students.

The night before, I heard a knock on my door at 10 pm and opened it. Before me was a tall bearded black teen who asked me if I wanted to party. I told him, "No, I can't even smoke because I have to run, and I have to study for an exam in the morning". He said, "It's free". I said, "No thanks, I've never done the stuff."

Seven short hours later, at 5 am, while I was getting in my final ZZZs, four things happened at once: there was a loud banging on the door, the banger announced very loudly SHERIFF!, the door was crashed open, and a Deputy appeared brandishing a pistol.

He then commanded me to sit down on the floor, which I gladly did. I was then presented with a search warrant.

My room was ransacked, culminating in the Deputy and his assistant pulling the carpet up. Nothing was found, not even a seed. This was miraculous. According to my boarding house neighbor, Earl. "Lots of dope was smoked in that room". Earl would know, as he was usually high. In the morning, we would chant to him "Hiii Earrrl!!!"

Earl was somewhat of an artist. He had painted a Picasso-like landscape in our hallway and named it Einstein's Vacation.

When the Sheriffs were finished with my room, they asked, "Are you coming with us or do we need to cuff you?"

I said, "I have seen a search warrant, do you have an arrest warrant?"

"Oh", the Deputy said. "I guess we don't."

They then clambered out of the boarding house, as other occupants in the building were rounded up.

So traumatized by the event, I couldn't sleep for a couple of nights. I then decided to move in with my friend Bobby down the street, who had lost a roommate that had turned out to be a murderer.

Bobby welcomed me in, as he always did.

As the last two months of the semester wound down, I heard about Bobby's former roommate who was incarcerated for double murder.

TAKE EVERYTHING (OR TOOK EVERYTHING)

Greg was a young successful lawyer. To be so, he was a workaholic. He was married, had three children and was in his mid-30s. Excitement, though, seemed to be missing.

Greg had an affair. Not just any affair but one with a woman of color, in poverty, who was 15 years younger. Betty was charming and smart, while also street savvy. She had four children, and had struggled all her life.

Greg met Betty through a friend. Greg helped Betty move away from an abusive boyfriend one Saturday. The mutual friend suggested that Betty and Greg might get to know each other better.

Indeed, they did. Greg and Betty would get together once every week or two and share a meal or more.

Greg kept the secret for five years. During this time, there were some red flags that he ignored. Betty did not have custody of her children. She had been married twice, and both husbands had been murdered. However, Betty was extremely well read and well spoken. Betty was beautiful and fun. So, Greg ignored the obvious.

The crossroad event happened when Greg visited Betty on the North side of town, a poor area that had crime. As Greg was unloading some groceries he had bought for Betty, three teenage boys began to march around Greg in a circle. Then, one broke off from the circle and put a pistol to the back of Greg's head. Greg fell to his knees and said, "Take everything."

They took Greg's wallet and fled.

Greg told Betty he had to go, and did.

Betty asked three male friends to help her. They recovered Greg's wallet, that was just missing the cash. One of Betty's friends encountered one of the suspects at a nearby Quick Stop and got some of the cash back.

Greg was very distraught and didn't know what to do.

Instead of taking the red flag for what it was, he decided he was having a John the Baptist Road to Damascus event: he had been knocked off of his saddle and needed to decide what to do about Betty. Greg decided that he wanted to marry Betty, and that this was some kind of a sign that he should. He therefore proposed to her and she accepted.

Greg left his wife of 32 years, divorced her, and fell out with his 3 sons.

He then picked out a house for Betty and moved in. However, Betty did not move in, but two of her children did, Julian age 18 and James age 23. Joining them was their cousin, Bradley.

Greg continued to plead with Betty to move in, now that they were married. Betty always had an excuse.

The two sons now living with Greg were distant with him. Bradley, however, befriended Greg. Bradley's Mother had some psychological issues and did not recognize him. He needed a parent figure. Bradley's Father also disowned him. A well-known drug pusher who had seen time, his Dad was out and dealing. The ritual was carefully guarded. He would leave drugs in a car at the top of his driveway with the backdoor only unlocked. Customers would drop off the money and take a bag. A nearby Pitbull watched the procedures.

Bradley and Greg began to go to church every Sunday. Finally, Bradley confided to Greg that Betty had an old boyfriend that she was living with. Bradley gave the address, which was near the gym where Greg worked out.

Greg went by the home site, and found the car that he had given to Betty.

Bradley was labeled a "Snitch". He was threatened by Betty and her two sons and had to move in with an Uncle who worked at Camp Pendleton in California. This turned out to be for the best. Bradley took a computer programming course, did well and has now "made it". He was never convicted of any crimes, unlike many of his relatives.

Greg met with the lawyer who had represented him in the divorce from his first wife and told her the story. The lawyer recommended that Greg divorce Betty immediately, as it sounded like the marriage was a sham.

Betty's allowance was cut off and the divorce proceeded. Betty approached Greg and asked if they could make up. With his lawyer's permission, Greg met with Betty and they discussed the situation. Greg was tempted, but said he would think about it.

Greg's eyes were really opened when, upon his lawyer's advice, he hired a private investigator to track Betty's activities. She and her boyfriend mingled a lot and took some questionable substances. That was not the worst part. The investigator was somewhat of a sadist. He called Greg "Casper". He'd also ask if Greg wanted to look at the videos that he was taking of Betty's activities. Greg was tempted to do so, but declined.

One night, Betty's son, Julian, was driving back to Greg's house for the evening, but was followed by a drug pusher that he apparently owed money to. As Julian entered the driveway, shots rang out, and five found their mark in the car, leaving bullet holes.

Frightened in the house, Greg had a reverse-Damascus event. He decided that Betty and her family were bad news.

The next day Greg had the locks to his house changed, got the police to help him convince the two sons to move out of the house and to live with their mother, and Greg never looked back.

The divorce has been final now for about 10 years, Greg is happily remarried and has decided that he does not want any more guns in his life.